To Sophie

Can't Catch Me!

John Prater

PUFFIN BOOKS

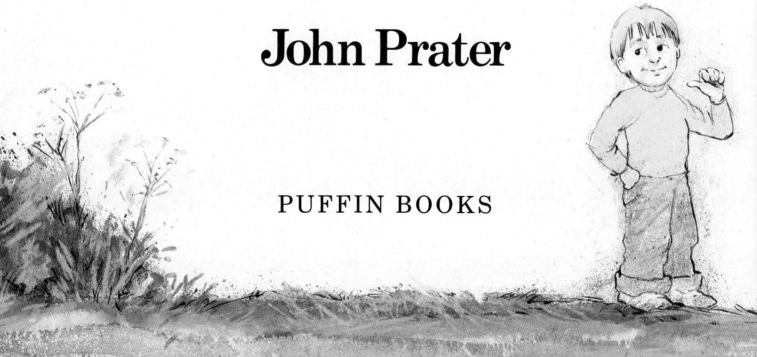

"It's bathtime, Jack," called Dad.
"I hate baths!" said Jack.

"Go and have your bath RIGHT NOW!"
said Mum.

"You can't catch me!" Jack replied.

And he set off down the garden.

"They're coming! I'll hide in here,"
thought Jack.

"He's in the shed!" shouted Mr Crabtree.

Jack slipped nimbly out of the window.

"Mind my vegetables!"
yelled Mr Crabtree as
he joined in the chase.

"You can't catch me!"
said Jack...

and he was right.

Mrs Polly was hanging out her washing.
"Mind my clean clothes!" she shrieked.

"You can't catch me!" said Jack...

and he was right.

"Mind my bike!" shouted Mr Digwood.
"You can't catch me!" said Jack,
as he dashed into the lane.

"Mind where you're going, boy!" warned
Colonel Watt as Jack sped past.

"You can't catch me!" said Jack...
and he was right.

Jack hid in the shadow of a large tree, while the angry grown-ups looked everywhere for him.

"You can't catch me!" he said to himself...

and he was right.

When the coast was clear,
Jack set off again.
"They'll never catch me!"
he thought, but…

Oh! What a mess!

Even worse, Jack couldn't move until
the grown-ups had passed.

"Still, they can't catch me!" he whispered
to his new friend, the pig, and he was right.

No one saw him plod home...

or what he did when he got there.

"Hello!" said Jack. "You
can't catch me!"
But this time, he was wrong.

Some other Picture Puffins